For Tre, TJ, Aaliyah and all types of Rainbow Learners who are In the Mix

AUTHOR'S NOTE: In the Mix is an expression to combine two or more things. It also suggests that the students are directly involved in the learning process. AJ the DJ is a cool teacher who engages his students through his differentiated instructional style of rhymes and music.

SUMMARY: Turn the page to find out how this cool teacher, AJ The DJ engages his students through various learning styles and "activate" and turn up their brain power in the classroom. Turning average learners into SUPER learners. 7 Flavors (Learning Styles) Pick 1, pick a few!

ISBN 978-0-578-20549-6

Note to Parents & Teachers:

This book includes a 7 Learning Styles Chart. Students make greater progress when given many opportunities to be who they wanna be, and use their areas of strengths or their special "mixes" to master learning standards in the class. This formula turns any student from an average learner to a Super Achiever!

7 Learning Styles Chart

Visual   **Musical**   **Verbal**   **Physical**

Mathematical   **Social**   **Solitary**

TRE AND TJ
IN THE MIX
TURN UP YOUR BRAIN POWER

Ka'Trina E. Cannon Holt

Illustrated by **Cameron Holmes**

Writeous Images, LLC

KCH

Charlie:
Hello Lit Camper!
Thanks for your
support!

Hi I'm a teacher by day and a DJ by night. Music helps me relax making my soul feel brighter than daylight. When I'm in the classroom, I love to mix teaching and music to help my students learn. I want every student to be successful that's my main concern.

3

Just like ice cream, learners come in many different flavors and styles. Sometimes a learner has just one style or a different mix. Your teacher is trained to help you pick and grant your wish!

YO, YO, YO, YO!
Tell me a little bit more about
all the many learning styles I
can use in school, so I can
follow the golden rule, be
smart, turn-up and be so cool.

**SO, SO, SO, SO! Oooh, I know!
Let me show you how I operate
so that you too can be great!**

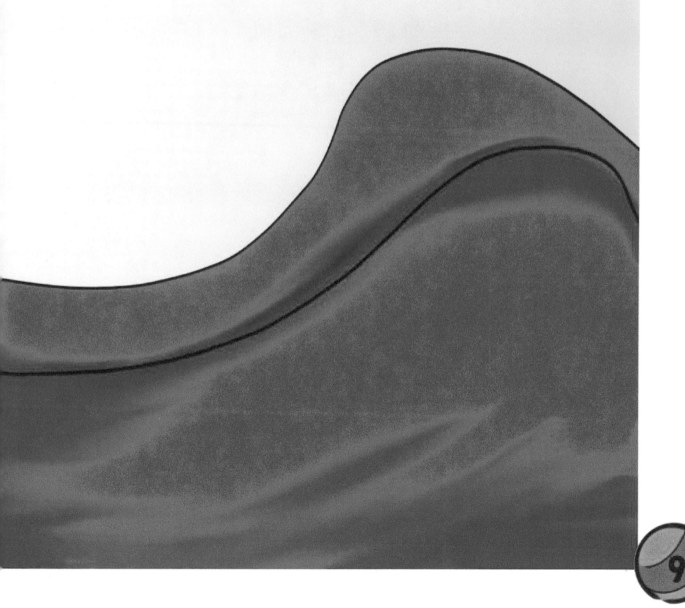

Look at this logo on
my chest.
Please watch how I
do this with so much
ease, style, and
finesse.

When I use manipulatives such as counters or building blocks, this helps me use my eyes to visualize, then I tap into my brain and realize, how to solve many answers that make me wise.

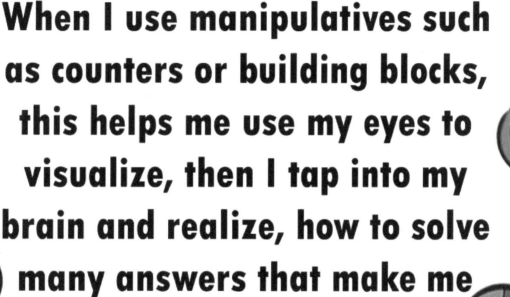

Then I know I can do my best, and I'm okay with taking this silly logo off my chest.

14

AYE, AYE, AYE, AYE!
Speak the letters you see
READY, SET, GO,
repeat after me
T-R-E,
Hey my friend that's the
person who I be, and
check out how I describe
this world around me.

I am mainly a visual learner and my teacher guides me with pictures and objects to help me be my best. It has nothing to do with super powers or having a logo on my chest.

Yes!
You are brilliant, Tre! There are seven learning styles and many teachers recognize that each student prefers to use different ways to learn called techniques. Wow so neat! Learn your style so that you can compete, and your state's learning standards you will master or meet!

Learning styles group common ways that students learn. Each student has his or her mix of styles. Some students may find that they have a stronger preferred style of learning, with far less use of the other styles--Oooh we child!

Give a cheer students did you just hear? There is no right mix, neither are your learning styles fixed!

OH, OH, OH, OH!
I get it now, Cuzzo!
Like you, I too, am in the mix!
Now Mr. DJ hear what I have
to say, let me do this thing my
way. Please hand me your bag
of tricks so I can be in the mix,
turn-up, and get my own
learning fix.

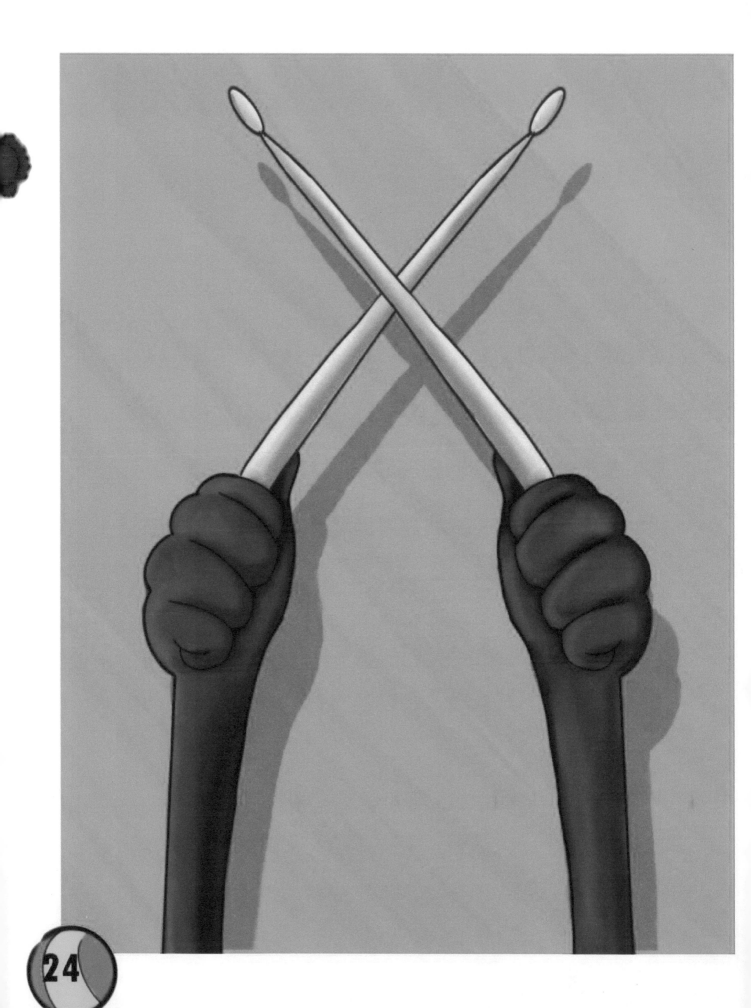

You see these two
drummer's sticks?
I use them to create a
perfect rhyme, that
helps me to stay
focused all the time.

I can study and look at
those words all day
long but I don't care.....
It's hard sitting still in
my chair, all I do is sit
and stare.
I sigh! I'm so tired,
Oh my, I cry!

But once I get in the mix,
and pick up my two sticks,
I come alive and get
energized, moving,
music and beats help me to
recall and memorize.

I can spell anything when I use my learning style to rap, make a beat or sing!

That's it TJ, don't quit! Look in my DJ bag and pull out some tricks to get your learning fix. Sometimes you won't be able to use your drummer's sticks or hands or feet to make a beat but don't give into defeat.

Use your imagination, your mind is big and round, use your spelling words and pretend you're giving a rap concert, the world is your stage - your audience won't let you down. You can silently Bee-Bop, rap or create a beat it doesn't matter if you're five or fifteen, you can use your imagination at any age.

YO, YO, YO, YO!
Check this out, I'm telling you
this works without a doubt.

Your spelling word is believe, now
don't panic no time to fret.
Remember the strategy I gave you
before the test.

Oh yeah, I remember it's I
before E, except after C.
Man, that short rhyme just
helped me to remember how to
spell believe. 1, 2, 3, easy,
breezy, peasy. I remember a
rhyme and used that as my
guide to ace the test.
"Ok Teach tell us what's next?"

WELL, WELL, WELL!
Deuces my learners!
That's it, I gotta split but
before I go, one thing I
wanna know which
learning style can you
get with? Come on ya'll
this is almost the end so
you better get lit!

My dear friends out there in Readers' Land! Are you like Tre, the Super Achiever who is mostly a visual learner and sometimes a logical learner? Perhaps, you are more like TJ, the mainly physical learner and sometimes sound learner who is in the mix with his rap beats, dance moves and his two drummer's sticks?

Feel free to create your own rap and tell us how you learn. You can write it, sing it, dance it, build it, record it, we don't care how you learn just get up and grab your DJ's bag, and get that A, by using your smart swag!

DEUCES! LEARNERS YOU ARE NOW IN THE MIX! STAY LIT

Yours Truly,
Teacher AJ the DJ

TRE AND TJ
IN THE MIX
TURN UP YOUR BRAIN POWER

7

About The Author

Ka'Trina Cannon Holt

Educator and Authorpreneur,
Ka'Trina Cannon Holt is passionate about teaching
and helping change average learners into super
learners. She is devoted to giving her readers
engaging, fun, rhythmic styled learning adventures
to help each reader get, "In the Mix, "Get Lit," and
"Turn Up" their brain power! Ms. Holt is an
educator for the Dekalb County Public School System
in GA. She is a proud mom of successful adult
children who are now lifelong super learners with
families of their own.

www.writeousness.com
writeousimages@hotmail.com
IG: astlrainbow
Twitter: astlrainbow
Facebook: astlrainbow

CPSIA information can be obtained
at www.ICGtesting.com
Printed in the USA
BVHW021212090620
581101BV00003B/36